Lizzy Has Fantastic Feet

By Antoinette Simmonds

Pictures by Ian Dale

INOT
PRODUCTIONS

LIZZY HAS FANTASTIC FEET
Published by INOT Productions

INOTproductions.com

Text © 2022 INOT Productions
Illustrations © 2022 Ian Dale

Library of Congress Control Number: 2022906708
ISBN (Hardcover) 978-1-7350295-3-5
ISBN (Paperback) 978-1-7350295-4-2
eISBN 978-1-7350295-5-9

First Edition 2022

Dedication

Lizzy Has Fantastic Feet is dedicated to my family and friends both near and far! With all the love, patience, and understanding they have extended, it has allowed me an opportunity to create and explore my thoughts and imagination. Thank you!

I'd like to extend a special "thank you" to my long-time friend, Michelle Thomas, for assisting me with the editing of *Lizzy Has Fantastic Feet*.

With God as my rock, I dedicate this book in memory of my dad, Houston, and mom, Roberta, who inspired me to pursue my dreams.

The butterfly represents my dad hovering over family and friends with words of encouragement and wisdom. The bird represents my mom who was an avid reader, a delightful storyteller, and a spontaneous, natural singer.

Keep the Faith

—Antoinette Simmonds

"Come play in the treehouse!" Caius shouted down to his brothers.

Looking up from below, Kendall said, "not yet. Dad said we have to clean up the leaves first!"

"And then Mom said we have to clean up our rooms!" Kayson added.

5

Caius flopped on his back. "I bet by the time they finish, they'll have forgotten all about me. No one ever wants to play with me."

Dad was always telling Caius to speak up more, but it was hard for him to find the words.

A tear rolled down Caius's cheek. He could feel a big cry coming, but just as he opened his mouth, he heard a sob…

Down below, the boys heard the noise, too!

"Are you crying, Caius?" they shouted.

Caius stuck his head out the window of the treehouse. "No, it's not me."

Next door, Kendall's friend Luis heard the commotion and came over to see what was happening.

"Shush!" Caius whispered, tiptoeing down the treehouse ladder and toward the noise.

The group spread out to follow the sound.

Suddenly, Caius spotted something. "I found it!"

"It's a lizard," Kendall said. He
and Luis started laughing.

"I see lizards all the time," Kayson said.

Disinterested, the three boys
started to walk away.

Then they heard the lizard
and Caius talking.

9

"I'm so lonely," the lizard said. "No one wants to play with me."

"I know how that feels," Caius said, looking at his brothers.

To his surprise, they turned and came back.

"Caius," Kendall said, "is that Lizard talking!?"

Caius nodded, then turned
back to the lizard.

"Why won't anyone play
with you?" he asked.

The lizard sniffled loudly, tears running
down her nostrils. "My feet are too big!"

The lizard stretched and showed her feet.

"Wow! You do have big feet!" said Caius. Just then, a rabbit popped out from a hole in the ground next to the treehouse. "Lizard, why are you crying?"

"No one wants to play with me because my feet are too big," the lizard said again.

Rabbit wiggled his nose and straightened his bow tie.

"Feet?" he asked. "You're worried about your feet? Phooey. Your grandfather, Colonel Arnold Lizard, had feet just like yours, and he did great things with them!"

"He did?" asked the lizard.

The rabbit eyed the lizard. "You don't know?" he asked.

The lizard shook her head.

"Why, he used his feet to protect the ants and baby lizards from the great storm. He held those feet up like an umbrella, and although the winds blew, Colonel Arnold kept them dry and safe."

At that, the lizard stopped crying.

"You're right. I have big feet and
I like them!" The rabbit gave a
firm nod and hopped away.

For a moment, the lizard sat up tall and proud. Then she slunk down again.

"But ... what if no storm comes? Then what will I do with my feet?"

The boys looked at each other.

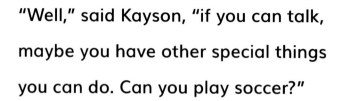

"Well," said Kayson, "if you can talk, maybe you have other special things you can do. Can you play soccer?"

Kendall spotted a ball and kicked it towards Caius.

Seeing the ball coming, the lizard stopped it with her foot.

"Whoa!" Caius said. "You stopped the ball! Can you do that with both feet?"

Rolling the ball back, the boys started kicking the ball to the lizard.

Surprised, Kendall shouted,

"This lizard has a powerful kick!"

Caius looked at the lizard and said, "I think you need a name. How about Lizzy?"

Lizzy nodded. She liked that.

The boys taught Lizzy how to play
all day, until it began to get dark.

Soon both moms called to have
the boys come inside.

Caius nodded. Picking up the ball,
he thought maybe Lizzy could
stay inside in their room.

So the boys told their Mom about
the lizard, and asked if they
could keep it in their room.

"Well, for some animals, the outside is
their home," Mom said. "Why don't we see
what Dad thinks when he gets home?"

Kendall, Kayson, and Caius looked up
and saw their dad coming in the yard.

The brothers all ran to him. "Dad,
can we keep Lizzy in the house?"

"Who's Lizzy?" asked Dad.

So, Caius pushed aside the
leaves, and there was Lizzy.

"Hi, guys, is it time to play
again?" she asked.

"A talking Lizard?" Dad said. "That's
something new. Let's plan on keeping
the lizard outside, and we can
camp in the back yard tonight."

"HOORAY!" Everyone
shouted and jumped for joy!

Happy, Caius lead the boys as the family gathered in the yard with blankets that night. Using his own words, Caius begins telling all about Lizzy and how he found her.

While Mom and Dad listened, Caius knew that he had always relied on his older brothers to do most of the talking, but now it was his turn to speak up.

And he did!

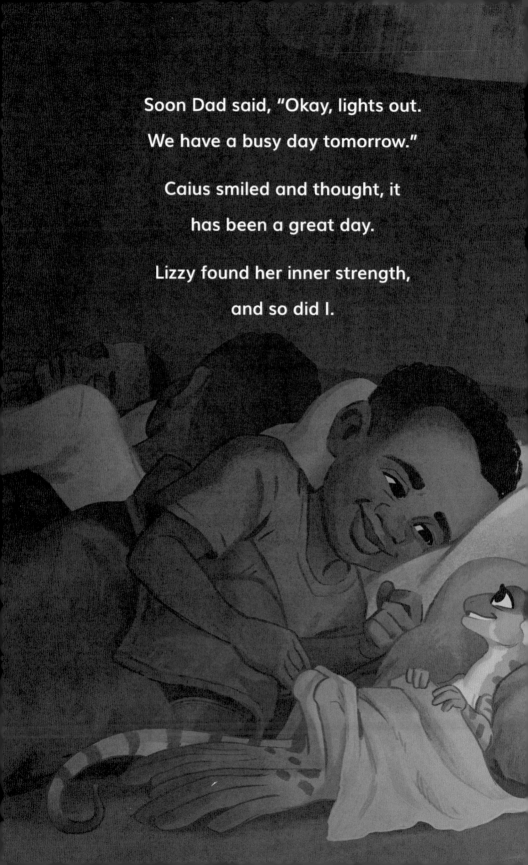

Soon Dad said, "Okay, lights out.
We have a busy day tomorrow."

Caius smiled and thought, it
has been a great day.

Lizzy found her inner strength,
and so did I.